This book belongs to:

FOUR LITTLE PUPPIES

Our Version of the Antique

© 1983 B. Shackman & Co., Inc.,
N.Y., N.Y. 10003
No.30439 Printed in Hong Kong

**Our Version
of the
Antique Original**

*Dedicated to all
the little puppies who posed for
the pictures in this book*

Once upon a time there were four little puppies. Their names were Wags, Tags, Rags, and Obadiah.

BASEBALL TO-DAY

They lived with their Uncle Oscar and their Aunt Abbie. Uncle Oscar taught them to keep busy. He taught them to bark at strange people. And he taught them to bury their bones neatly.

Aunt Abbie taught them to help others. She taught them to wag their tails. And she taught them never *never* NEVER to chase kittens.

One day Wags and Tags and Rags and Obadiah were out in the back yard. They were very busy. They were sweeping the leaves off the sidewalk.

Pretty soon Tags stopped working. She scratched her nose.

"Woof!" said Tags. "I am tired of working. I am going into the kitchen to make myself a nice bone stew."

And she did.

Wags and Rags and Obadiah went right on working. They dug in the garden and made the dirt fly. And they pulled out weeds.

Pretty soon Rags stopped working.

He scratched his left ear.

"Woof!" said Rags. "I am tired of working. I am going to put on my best suit and play drum—*rub-a-dub-dub!"*

And he did.

Wags and Obadiah went right on working.

Pretty soon Obadiah stopped.

He scratched his right ear.

"Woof!" said Obadiah. "I am tired of working. I am going to listen to my favorite crooner on the radio and read *Puppies, Just Puppies.*"

And he did.

Wags was left all by himself.

But he was a good puppy! He kept right on working. He put on his hat and went up and down the street, selling his copies of *Dog Life, the Puppies' Own Magazine.*

After that, Wags went to the market for Aunt Abbie. He bought a new broom. He bought a new potato masher. He bought a soup bone and a pound and a half of Hamburg steak.

After that, Wags made some nice pan-
cakes for Aunt Abbie. They tasted good!

After that, Wags practiced his banjo lesson.

He practiced all his scales.

He practiced his one-paw exercises. And he practiced his new piece, "Bone, Sweet Bone."

After Wags had done all his work, he wanted someone to play with him.

Tags was listening to the radio. Rags was playing the drum. Obadiah was reading *Puppies, Just Puppies*. They did not want to play with him.

So Wags went out and barked for Teeny, the puppy next door.

"*Yip!*" called Wags. "Come and play!"

But the puppy next door did not answer.
She was taking her afternoon nap.

So Wags barked for Fido and Fritz who lived next door to Teeny.

"*Yip, yip!*" called Wags. "Come and play!"

But Fido and Fritz did not answer. They were taking a drive in their new dog cart.

Wags barked again.

"*Yip, yip, yip!*"

But nobody heard him except two strange puppies marching by. And they just stared and said nothing.

Wags barked again.

"*Yip, yip, yip, yip!*"

But nobody heard him except the Widow Bingo, who was working in her garden.

"*Sh!*" said the Widow Bingo.   "Puppies should be seen and not heard."

Wags stopped barking and put on his mud-pie suit. He pushed his wagon around the yard.

Pretty soon he felt a tug at his blouse.

He turned around.

And there was a little yellow kitten!

"*Mew!*" said the kitten. "Will you do me a favor?"

"Certainly," said Wags, who was always polite. And he wagged his tail once.

"Then," said the kitten, "please lift me up so that I can mail this letter."

So Wags lifted her up to the mail box and she mailed her letter.

And the kitten purred.

"Mew!" said the kitten. "Will you do me *another* favor?"

"Certainly," said Wags. And he wagged his tail twice.

"Then," said the kitten, "let's dress up and you pretend to be my mother. And read me a bedtime story."

So Wags and the kitten changed their clothes and Wags read her *Four Little Kittens.* And the kitten purred.

"Mew!" said the kitten. "Will you do me *another* favor?"

"Certainly," said Wags. And he wagged his tail three times, though he *was* getting a little tired.

"Then," said the kitten, "please take me home. Lena, my hound nurse, doesn't like me to cross the street alone."

So Wags and the kitten crossed the street together. And the kitten purred.

At the kitten's home, Wags found Lena feeding the kitten's littlest sisters.

She thanked Wags for bringing the kitten home.

"I'm glad to see you do not chase kittens," said Lena. "Drop in for a bone stew sometime. Thursday is my day off."

Wags said he would. He thought Lena had beautiful ears.

When Wags got home, Tags and Rags and Obadiah were all ready to sing songs.

So they sang "Old Dog Tray" and "Three Blind Mice."

Wags sang the loudest.

After a while, Uncle Oscar came home.
"Wags! Tags! Rags! Obadiah!"
he barked. "Come here!"

So Wags, Tags, Rags, and Obadiah came and stood before him.

Uncle Oscar shook his head sadly when he looked at Tags and Rags and Obadiah.

"Lazy pups!" he said. "Your aunt told me how you spent the day. No bones for your supper. Now GET TO WORK!"

So Tags and Rags and Obadiah got to work. They raked up all the leaves and carted them out to the alley. They took turns riding back.

They worked for a long, long time.

Wags got an extra bone for his supper.
And he got a ride in an airplane, too!
He was a good puppy.

**Did You Enjoy
This Story ?
Good !
Now Go To Sleep**